The MOFFATTS on the Road

All for One and One for All

By Nancy Krulik

SCHOLASTIC INC.

New York Toronto London Auckland Sydney
Mexico City New Delhi Hong Kong

For Amanda and Ian, who are
always there for each other.

ISBN 0-439-13688-1

William Bell & Associates, Inc.
Personal Management — Nashville, TN

12 11 10 9 8 7 6 5 4 3 2 1   0 1 2 3 4 5 6/0

Printed in the U.S.A.
First Scholastic printing, August 2000

Chapter One

"Here they come!"

As soon as the girl in the blue bell-bottoms and white half-shirt spotted the Moffatts' tour bus turning into the parking lot, she ran at top speed to greet the guys. She'd been waiting for hours to come face-to-face with her favorite pop group, and now that they were finally within her line of vision, she couldn't control herself. She *had* to see them up close.

Her friends had been waiting just as long and were equally blown away by the excitement of seeing the tour bus coming toward them. Within seconds, the bus was surrounded by breathless, impatient girls, each hoping to get the attention of her favorite member of the group. Some of the teens carried signs that welcomed the Moffatts. Others wore Moffatts T-shirts and baseball caps. Still others were carrying portable stereos and blasting Moffatts songs into the atmosphere.

But they all had one thing in common. Each one of them began screaming at the top of her lungs the minute the Moffatts' bus came into view.

"What's goin' on here?" Bob Moffatt asked as he looked out the bus window at the throngs of shouting teens.

Usually, Bob wouldn't have been at all surprised at the sight of screaming fans. After all, now that the Moffatts had become a multinational pop sensation, girls always greeted the guys before a concert. But tonight's show was different. It was a secret. No one in the general public was supposed to have known that the guys were even *in* Bordentown, Illinois. So Bob couldn't imagine why all these fans were lined up waiting for them.

"I thought you said we were only going to play a small gig for the local press," Scott Moffatt called up to the front of the bus where his dad, Frank, was sitting. "Invitation only."

"It *is* an invitation-only performance," Frank assured his eldest son. "Only about fifty people — newspaper reporters, local TV anchors, and DJs from the greater Chicago area. This show is just for people who cover the local pop music scene for the press. And they were all under strict orders not to release information about the time and location of the performance."

"Then where'd all these girls come from?" Scott asked. "They don't look like reporters to me."

"Hey, don't look a gift horse in the mouth," Dave Moffatt scolded his older brother playfully. "I don't care where these lovely ladies came from. I'm just glad they're here!"

Scott had to laugh. Of his three younger triplet brothers, Dave was the one who was the most girl-crazy!

Before Frank could even venture a guess as to how the fans had gotten wind of the show, a short chubby man, who looked to be about 30 years old, pushed his way through the throngs of screaming teens and banged on the bus door.

"Lemme in!" he shouted. "It's me, Joey Sloane. I run this club."

The bus driver looked to Frank for his approval. Frank nodded, and the driver quickly opened the door and let Joey on board the bus. A bunch of girls tried to follow, but the door shut before they could push their way on board.

"What's going on here?" Joey demanded of the Moffatts. "Your booking agent told me this was supposed to be a private party. It was going to be kept quiet. Now I've got all these girls here begging me for tickets to a concert. My club can't hold all these kids. It's just a small hall. That's what we have here in Bordentown — small clubs, no big arenas like you guys usually play in. This *isn't* Chicago, y'know. We're just a suburb."

Frank nodded. "I can see that we have a little problem here," he agreed.

Joey stared at Frank in disbelief. "A *little* problem?" he exclaimed as he looked out on the crowd. "Do you see how many girls are out there?!"

But Frank was not the type to get upset easily. "It was also my understanding that this was a private affair," he continued calmly. "I promise you, *we* didn't put any ads or announcements about it in the papers, and the DJs have all assured me that they wouldn't mention the event on the air. I don't know how the fans learned about it."

"Only one way to find out," Clint Moffatt began as he opened the window nearest his bunk. "Gotta ask the girls."

As soon as the window opened, a sea of arms reached up. The girls pushed autograph books and pens at Clint. He grabbed the first one he saw and quickly signed his name on the page.

"So how'd you find out about this concert anyway?" Clint asked the owner of the autograph book. He took care to speak in his most nonchalant voice. He didn't want to upset the fans by telling them that there wasn't going to be a concert that night.

"It's on your web site," a teenage girl with short, curly red hair and big green eyes told him.

"I always check your site at least once a week to find out what you guys are doing. I couldn't believe it when it said you were going to be in Bordentown. As soon as I found out about the show, though, I borrowed my mom's car and drove almost an hour to get here. I've been waiting in this parking lot for ages. We all have. Do you know when they're going to start letting us buy tickets?"

Clint smiled politely, but since he didn't really have an answer for her at the moment, he just shrugged.

Bob, Dave, and Scott sooned joined Clint and signed autographs for a few more minutes. Then the brothers finally had to close the windows to try to figure out a solution to this dilemma. "Sorry, we'll try to give out more autographs in a few minutes," Clint told the disappointed fans as he shut the window closest to his bunk.

Scott went up to the front of the bus and turned on the family computer. He typed in **www.themoffatts.com** and waited for the group's web site to boot up. Suddenly, the Moffatts' logo flashed on the screen, along with pictures of the guys in concert, and e-mail messages from some of their fans. Scott moved the cursor to the section marked TOUR SCHEDULE and clicked the mouse. Instantly a list of dates appeared.

"Oh, man," Scott moaned. "She's right. There

it is." He pointed to the screen. "'Live show. Eight o'clock, the Keyboard Club, Bordentown, Illinois.'" he read aloud.

"How'd that get on there?" Dave wondered. "So much for keeping low-pro."

"We did give our web master a copy of our schedule," Clint mused. "This gig must have been on the list of shows. I guess he didn't realize it was supposed to be a private event."

"Well, *now* what are we supposed to do?" Bob asked his brothers. He looked at the sea of excited, faithful, beautiful faces that surrounded the bus. "We can't let those girls down."

"Well, you can't bring them in my club, either," Joey Sloane interrupted. "I've got a limit of a hundred and fifty people — max. There must be five hundred kids out there. The fire marshall'd close me down if I tried to bring 'em all inside."

"We'll just have to tell the fans that there's no show tonight. I don't see that we have any choice. I'll go out and try to explain this mix-up to them, and hope they'll understand," Frank told his sons.

"Oh, man! When you tell those girls that you guys aren't going to play for them, they'll tear my club apart," Joey groaned.

"Wait a minute, I've got an idea!" Dave announced suddenly. He turned to Joey. "The fire marshall doesn't have any rule about how many people can hang out in your parking lot does he?"

Joey shook his head. "No. Why?"

"Well, we still have two hours before the press shows up. And we're here for a rehearsal. Why not just have the rehearsal out here?"

Clint reached up and gave his brother a high five. "Awesome idea, bro!" he agreed. "Sort of an impromptu jam session."

Bob, the third triplet in the family, grabbed his drumsticks and headed for the front of the bus. "I'll bring my drum kit outside," he told the others. "You guys start looking for some extra-long extension chords. We've got a show to do!"

Chapter Two

"Hello Bordentown! It's great to see you!" Scott Moffatt shouted out to the sea of screaming girls in the parking lot. "We're the Moffatts."

At the very sound of the group's name, the fans went wild. Scott grinned and picked up his guitar. "Here's a song from our album. We wrote it, so we really hope you like it. If you do, let us know — 'cause life's too short to keep your emotions in!"

And with that, Dave placed his fingers solidly on his keyboard and played the opening notes to "If Life Is So Short." His brothers quickly chimed in — Scott on lead guitar, Clint on bass, and Bob on drums. The guys may have been using this live performance as a dress rehearsal, but to the fans, the music seemed as good as a real performance could be. Which was, of course, exactly as the guys had hoped.

The guys sang out to the crowd. But there

was no way to know whether or not the teens even heard the heartfelt lyrics to the romantic love song the Moffatts were playing. The girls were screaming, shouting, and singing along at the top of their lungs, so they could never have heard all the complicated harmonies and chord changes the song required. But the Moffatts were okay with that; they liked it when their concerts were audience-participation events.

Because they were all about the same age — teens, that is — the Moffatts' fans totally related to the message the guys were singing about. When the audience sang along with the Moffatts' lyrics, or wrote the brothers letters saying how much the Moffatts' music meant to them, the guys were keenly aware that they had formed a relationship with their listeners. And from the sound of the applause that followed the last notes of "If Life Is So Short," that was *exactly* what was happening here in the parking lot of the Keyboard Club.

But giving a concert for the press was another matter entirely. The members of the media were adults, and listening to a Moffatts' show was part of their job. And because they were journalists, the press usually tried to act restrained during a show — just to show how professional they were. The guys were going to have to play their hearts out to get a rise out of them.

So having the fans cheer for their music during

this impromptu outdoor jam session turned out to be great for the Moffatts. It helped psych them up for the difficult gig that they had to perform in less than two hours.

The Moffatts played six songs for the outdoor crowd. Then Clint leaned in toward the mike and announced, "We've got to run now."

But the huge group of teens who had gathered outside weren't having any of *that*. "More Moffatts! More Moffatts!" they shouted.

"Let's give 'em what they asked for," Scott whispered to his brothers. He turned to the crowd. "Okay, one more song," he agreed. "Then we've got to break up this party!"

Bob clicked his drumsticks together. "One, two, a-one-two-three-four!" he shouted. Then he gave the downbeat and started singing "Written All Over My Heart."

The Moffatts sang their hearts out on the encore. And when it came to a close they took their bows gratefully. Then the brothers turned and went inside, leaving the Keyboard Club's security team with the tough task of sending the fans home.

"That was soooo cool!" Dave exclaimed as he went into the backstage dressing room and started to search through his suitcase for the black cotton crewneck sweater he planned to wear for the press show.

"Yeah, if it goes half as well for the media, the reviews will be awesome," Bob agreed as he combed his long brown hair in front of the mirror.

The Moffatts all believed that making their fans happy was the main reason they performed. But the guys also knew that without having the press in your corner, you *had* no career. Whether or not it was fair, people did depend on reviewers to tell them if someone's music was worth spending money on. The radio people had to like the Moffatts music as well — without DJ support the fans would never get to hear their songs on the radio. And even though the Moffatts were a well-established act on the top 40 scene, they had to keep up those relationships. There were always new groups on the horizon who would be more than glad to have their records played in place of the Moffatts' songs.

"We'd better hurry up and change. We've got to run an indoor sound check, and the DJs and reporters will be here any minute," Scott reminded the others, sounding every bit like an older brother.

It was almost 11:30 when the Moffatts finished the private press show they'd originally come to do. They quickly packed up their clothes and instruments, and helped the road crew load everything back onto the bus. But even after putting on two totally energetic shows, the guys weren't tired at all. In fact, they were pumped up — running on pure adrenaline. So they kept on singing in four-part harmonies, even as they walked out the door.

"Sorry about the mix-up," Bob told Joey Sloane as they left the club.

"That's okay," Joey assured him. "That outdoor show'll be good publicity for the club. Making nice with the community and all that. By the way, you guys really rock!"

Scott patted his guitar case. "Thanks."

As the bus pulled away and headed for a nearby hotel, the brothers hung out on Scott's bunk.

"So what do you think they'll write about us?" Dave asked the others.

"I think the DJs liked it," Bob said. "And the newspaper people seemed to be smiling a lot, too. Some of them were even singing along with that last chorus of 'Girl of My Dreams.'"

Clint smirked. "Well, no matter what they write, I know we were hot tonight. Besides, what I'm really looking forward to is that show we're doing *tomorrow* night," he told his brothers. "The one at Sugar Mountain Amusement Park."

Scott laughed. "Isn't that where you're supposed to meet your blind date from the 'Win a Date with Clint Moffatt' contest they ran in *Teen Scream* magazine?"

"She'd have to be blind to want a date with a dog like you," Bob teased his brother.

Clint had to laugh. Considering he and Bob were identical twins, Bob had just ranked on himself!

"Well, if she's anything like that girl who won a chance to go on that shopping spree with us last May, you'll be okay," Scott recalled. "She was really sweet."

"And cute," Clint added. "Not to mention the fact that she had great taste in music — we were her favorite group!"

"Well, I'm just looking forward to riding the roller coasters," Dave interrupted. "And if some sweet girl is scared on the ride, I'll be more than glad to hold her hand through the whole ordeal."

Scott frowned and shook his head. Dave was such a flirt. "I heard they've got the world's fastest roller coaster," he commented, trying to change the subject. "And that their Himalaya is amazing."

"Sounds like you guys have a big day planned for yourselves," the guys' stepmother, Sheila, called back from her seat in the front of the bus. "So as soon as we hit the hotel, I want you guys to get some sleep. No jamming, no songwriting. Just lights out."

Dave yawned. That wasn't going to be a problem. Suddenly, he was getting tired. Besides, the sooner they all went to bed, the sooner they'd get up. And Dave wanted to leave extra early, so he could spend as much time as possible at Sugar Mountain Amusement Park.

When they reached the hotel, Scott followed the bellhop up to the suite while his brothers waited in the lobby for Frank and Sheila to check the family in. After the porter left the room, Scott walked into one of the two bedrooms and placed his overnight bag on a bed. He put Bob's bag on the bed beside his. Then he went into the next room and placed Dave and Clint's bags on their beds.

The triplets came up about ten minutes later. They looked exhausted. As soon as he heard his brothers enter the suite, Scott walked out into the living room area and greeted them. "Well, you guys heard Sheila," he told his younger brothers. "We'd better hit the sack. I put your stuff in that room with mine, Bob. Clint, you and Dave are in the other room."

Scott went into his room. When he was ready, he turned out the light and got into bed. Bob tried to do the same — except for some reason he *couldn't* get into his bed. The minute he crawled under the covers, his knees were crammed up around his chin. And no matter how hard he tried, there was no way he could straighten them.

"What's goin' on here?" Bob shouted as he tried again and again to ram his foot under the top sheet.

Finally, Bob stood up and stripped the blanket off the bed. He quickly discovered that the top sheet had been folded in half and tucked in. "Hey! Who short-sheeted my bed?" he demanded.

Clint and Dave came running, but Bob knew right away that they weren't the culprits. From the huge smile on Scott's face, there was only one brother who could have pulled this stunt.

"Very funny," Bob congratulated Scott. He began to remake the bed so he could go to sleep. "But if I were you, I wouldn't be so smug. Two can play at this game you know."

Dave and Clint looked at each other and shook their heads. They knew exactly what they were witnessing — the start of an old-fashioned practical joke war.

"May the best Moffatt win," Clint whispered quietly to Dave as the brothers headed back to their room.

Chapter Three

The next morning, the triplets were up early. But Scott had gotten a jump on them.

After breakfast at the hotel restaurant, Clint, Dave, and Bob raced out to the bus — only to discover that their big brother, Scott, was nowhere to be found.

"Man, where'd he wander off to?" Bob asked.

"I want to get out of here," Dave mumbled.

"You're not the only one," Clint agreed. "We've got a big day ahead of us."

Frank and Sheila walked to the parking lot together. "Okay, we're all checked out," Frank told his sons. "Everybody ready to go?"

"Everyone but Scott," Dave replied as he glanced down at his watch. "He's disappeared. Any chance we could just leave without him? I want to beat the crowds in line at the Double Looper and Triple Terror roller coasters."

"Nice try," Frank laughed. "But I think the

fans might notice if our lead guitarist wasn't there for the show."

"I wonder where he could have gone? It's not like him to be late," Sheila thought out loud.

Just then, Scott came racing up to his family. He held a newspaper in each of his hands.

"Sorry," he apologized. "I ran all over Borden-town trying to find a newsstand that was open early. I wanted to see the reviews of our show last night. Here they are — hot off the press!"

"Whoa! I was so into this amusement-park gig that I almost forgot all about that," Clint admitted. "What'd they say about us?"

Before Scott could answer, Frank put his arms around his eldest son and steered him toward the door of the bus. "You can read them while we ride," he told him. "Let's get *this* show on the road."

As the bus pulled away, the brothers gathered around Scott's bunk. Scott opened the Chicago paper first and read aloud.

" 'Talk about nice guys,' " Scott began reading. " 'When a big group of fans found out they could not get into the press-only Moffatts' show at the Keyboard Club last night, the guys decided to give the teens an impromptu free perfor-mance. This reporter didn't get to hear that show, but if the kids were treated to anything like the press performance that followed, they were really lucky. . . .' "

The article continued, listing the songs that the Moffatts had played at the press show, and closed by saying, "'It's obvious that the Moffatts love performing. That's a good thing, because it seems they have a long, successful career ahead of them.'"

Clint stood up and took a goofy bow. "Thank you, thank you, thank you," he joked. "No applause, just throw money."

Instead of cash, Scott threw his pillow at Clint's head.

"What's the other one say?" Bob asked, pointing to the second paper.

Scott picked up the local newspaper, the *Bordentown Courier-Post*, and turned to the Arts & Leisure section. "Here it is," he said. "It's shorter than the other one, but the headline is "'Brothers Make Beautiful Music Together.'"

Scott scanned the article quickly. "This woman says 'The Moffatts blend beautiful harmonies and strong, pop melodies together to create a sound that is distinctly their own. They are energetic and exciting in concert, which may explain why their female fans insist on seeing them again and again.'" Scott stopped reading for a second and started to chuckle.

"What's so funny?" Dave asked.

Scott stifled a giggle. "You guys won't believe what she wrote next," he told the others.

"What?" Clint insisted. "Come on. Give."

"Listen to this," Scott looked down at the paper again. "'The brothers are all professional and wonderfully gifted. But one Moffatt brother is a true standout. We'll be expecting big things from Dave Moffatt in the future, since he appears to have the charisma and charm that will take him far in any entertainment genre.'"

"O-o-o, Dave," Bob needled his brother. "I think that reporter has a crush on you."

"Your charisma is like a magnet," Clint teased. He grabbed Dave around the leg and pretended to be attached to his limb. "I can't break free of the power."

"And what about his *charm*?" Scott added sarcastically, goofing on Dave. "I'm so drawn to you! Like a moth to a flame."

Dave laughed out loud. "You're all just jealous of my singular talent," he shot back as he shook Clint loose.

After a while, Dave's brothers quit their ribbing, and the Moffatts settled in on their bunks for the two-hour drive to the park, listening to tapes and reading books.

"Hey you guys, check this out — they're playing a whole afternoon of Beatles tunes on this oldies station," Bob alerted his brothers. He looked down at the radio dial on his Walkman. "I don't know the name of the station, but it's located at ninety-eight point two."

The others moved the dials on their personal

stereos so that they were all listening to the same tunes. And before long, Clint, Scott, and Bob were all happily singing along with the *original* fab four. "Baby you can drive . . ."

Only Dave was silent. Ordinarily by now, he'd have grabbed a hairbrush, pretending it was a microphone — doing some goofy lounge-singer act that always had his brothers laughing so hard that they were rolling in the aisles. But today, Dave sat silently on his bunk, staring out the window as the bus rolled along the highway on its way to Carlisle, Ohio, home of the Sugar Mountain Amusement Park.

He couldn't help it. That review from the newspaper dominated his thoughts.

Dave knew that the article was just one person's opinion. But try as he might, Dave couldn't put the woman's words out of his mind. Personal praise was new to him. He'd never been singled out before. He'd always been one of the Moffatts, or at the very most, one of the triplets. No one had ever specifically written about his musical skills in a newspaper article or review before. But this time he wasn't one of the pack. He was the standout. And Dave had to admit the obvious: It felt really good to be noticed.

Chapter Four

Two hours later, as the Moffatts tour bus pulled into the Sugar Mountain Amusement Park's artist parking lot, the guys looked up to see a giant billboard promoting their concert at the park. In the humongous image, the guys were all smiling broadly. Scott was in the front of the picture, Bob and Clint were standing nearby at Scott's right, with their arms around each other's shoulders. Dave was off to the left on his own.

Dave grinned as he glanced at the billboard. He thought he looked pretty good up there. He ran his fingers through his hair. *Even on a billboard, I have a certain charisma*, he thought to himself. *Your eye goes right to me, even though there are four people on the sign.*

Dave didn't say out loud what he was thinking. He knew his brothers would rag on him — big time. So he just beamed happily to himself.

Whatever it *is*, he thought. *I have it!*

*　　*　　*

As soon as the bus was parked behind the
stage, the guys began helping the stage crew
unload the instruments, amps, cords, and micro-
phones that would be needed for the concert
that night. Dave rushed to get his keyboard set
up, and then stood behind it, fingering a new
melody that was running through his head.

"Hey, you want to give us a hand over here?"
Clint asked from behind a huge soundboard that
was placed in the center of the amphitheater, di-
rectly across from the stage. "You're not the only
one in the group you know. Everyone's equipment's got to be set up before we can rehearse."

Dave sighed. It was just like his brothers to interrupt his creative process because they needed
help. But he didn't argue. That would have just
wasted more time. He turned off his electric
keyboard, and ambled over to help Bob set up
his drum kit.

After about a half an hour, the stage was
ready. "Hey, how about we go out into the park
for a while, and then have a rehearsal?" Bob
suggested to his brothers. "It's still early, so we
won't get stuck on any lines at the rides."

Just then Frank walked up to the stage. "Nice
try," he told his long-haired son. "But no dice.
Finish your work and then you can spend the entire afternoon on the roller coaster."

Scott smiled. "Okay if we go to a food stand and grab a quick bite first? I'm starving."

Frank laughed. His sons always seemed to be starving. And since the catering people who provided the food for the Moffatts had only just arrived, he nodded. "But I want you four back here in twenty minutes for a rehearsal. Got it?"

"Got it!" the guys all said in unison. Then they ran off to the nearest food stand and ordered four burgers with everything.

Bob was the first to get his food. He went to the far corner of the lunch area and grabbed a table for the others. Luckily it was early in the day, and no one was eating. Usually, Bob loved hanging out with the fans who inevitably recognized them at every fast-food place they stopped at, but today the guys only had twenty minutes. That would never be enough time to sign autographs, chat, and manage to wolf down a meal.

"This place is awesome," Clint said as he took his tray and scooted down on the bench beside his brother. "Did you see the size of the Triple Terror?"

"I want to check out that water slide that's completely enclosed in a dark tube. I think it's called the Black Hole," Bob replied.

"Sounds good to me," Scott remarked as he and Dave took seats on the bench across from their brothers. "Water slides are the coolest.

There's another one called Niagra Falls. I'll go with you after rehearsal. Pass the salt, please?"

Scott grabbed the shaker from Bob's hand and turned it upside down over his fries. *Pow!* A mountain of salt landed in the middle of Scott's plate, covering his fries and his burger. Someone had unscrewed the shaker top!

It didn't take long for Scott to figure out who the culprit was. Bob was laughing so uncontrollably that soda was coming out of his nose!

"Gotcha!" Bob said between snorting giggles. "You should have seen your face when that salt poured out."

"Very funny!" Scott scowled at his younger brother. "Now my food's ruined." He glanced at his watch. "And I don't even have time to order another burger."

"What a spoilsport you are," Bob complained. "Can't you take a joke?"

Scott smirked sweetly at Bob. "Oh sure I can, dude," Scott assured him, his voice dripping with sarcasm. "The question is, can *you*?!"

Clint listened with amusement to his brothers' one-ups.

"What do you think Scott is going to do next?" Clint whispered to Dave.

But Dave didn't answer. He was too busy thinking about something far more urgent.

*　　*　　*

As soon as they returned to the amphitheater, Scott, Bob, and Clint went up onto the stage. Scott sat on a stool and began tuning his guitar. Clint did the same with his bass. Bob moved the cymbals closer to his chair and kicked the foot pedal near his bass drum.

Dave didn't take his traditional spot behind the keyboards. He sat down on a bleacher in the front row and stared off into space.

"Hey, what's up with you?" Clint called down. "Come up here and start playing. The sooner we rehearse, the faster we can ride the roller coasters."

"And the quicker you get to meet your mystery woman," Scott laughed as he poured himself a drink from a pitcher of ice tea sitting on a nearby table. Someone had left a whole shelf of condiments on the table as well — sugar, lemons, salt, and pepper. Scott squeezed a lemon into his drink.

Clint grinned. "Her name's Teresa Rodriguez. It's such a cool name. I'll bet she's awesome, too. I wonder if she's tall or small, or medium height, or . . ."

Bob walked over toward the table, poured himself a glass of ice tea, and picked up the sugar. "Come on, you don't really care what she looks like," Bob said. "You just care that she liked you enough to enter that contest!"

Clint laughed. "What's not to like? Besides, at least I know she has good taste in guys!"

Bob took a sip of ice tea — and instantly spit it out onto the floor. "Her taste is certainly better than this," he gagged.

Scott started laughing. "What? You don't like salt in your ice tea?"

Bob grimaced. "So *that's* what that awful flavor is!" He looked curiously at his older brother. "Hey. How did you know there was salt in my ice tea?"

"Who do you think filled the sugar dispenser with salt?" Scott answered with a mischievous grin. "I made the switch while you were busy discussing Clint's love life."

"Listen you guys, I hate to interrupt this conversation, but I gotta talk to you," Dave interrupted. He walked slowly onto the stage. "This is serious."

"What's up?" Scott asked as a look of concern flashed over his face. "Are you feeling sick or something?"

Dave shook his head. "No. I feel fine. It's just that I've been thinking that, well . . . er . . . you see . . ."

"Spit it out, Dave," Bob urged. "We don't have all day. Just say what's on your mind."

"Well, I'd like to try going out on my own for a while," Dave blurted out quickly.

"That's cool," Scott replied with a shrug. "We

can all go our separate ways in the park after rehearsal. No big deal."

Dave shook his head. "No. I mean I want to *perform* on my own. As a solo act. That woman reporter thought I could make it on my own. And you guys don't really need a keyboardist. A lot of groups just have a guitar, a bass, and drums."

Bob started laughing. "Good one, Dave! Wish I'd thought of that practical joke."

Dave shook his head. "No joke."

At first, the other three Moffatts just stared at Dave. And then it hit them like an ice-cold splash of water: Their brother wasn't kidding. All at once, they all erupted.

"Are you nuts?" the usually calm Bob screamed. "We've been a group since we were little kids. You can't split up the act. We've worked together forever. That's how it's always been."

"Just because that's how it's always been, doesn't mean it's how it'll always have to be," Dave countered.

"You're not going anywhere!" Scott added. "The fans expect *four* Moffatts onstage. If you split, we'll be breaking our contract with Sugar Mountain — and with the rest of the venues on this tour."

"What kind of brother are you?!" Clint demanded.

"Dad'll never let you leave us in the lurch like this!" Bob assured his brother.

But Bob was wrong.

For just then, Frank Moffatt, who'd slipped onto the stage without his sons noticing, stepped in to break up the argument.

"Dave, are you sure this is what you want to do?" he asked his son gently.

Dave looked away from his brothers' angry glares. "Yes, Dad, I am. That reporter said I have what it takes to be a solo act. I've got to give it a try. I owe that to myself."

"But what do you owe *us*?" Scott demanded. He pointed to the empty bleachers in the amphitheater. There were enough seats for 2,000 people. And the Sugar Mountain Amusement Park manager expected every seat in the house to be filled that night. "You didn't get to play big theaters like this by yourself, you know."

Frank put a calming hand on Scott's shoulder. "Well, Scott, tonight Dave is going to take this stage on his own," he told the guys, "as your opening act. That way, all four Moffatts will perform. We won't be breaking any contracts."

Scott, Bob, and Clint couldn't believe what they had just heard. What was their dad saying? Did he honestly think it was okay for Dave to leave the group? After all they'd been through together?

When the four Moffatt boys were little (Scott was six and the triplets were five), they'd all gotten together to record a song for their grandfather. It was the first recording they'd ever made, but even back then, the brothers had all agreed that it wasn't going to be the last. They'd been bitten by the show-biz bug.

With the help of their dad, the guys had learned some songs and a few dance moves and began traveling around Canada, singing as a group. Over the years they'd driven thousands of miles on the tour bus, living practically on top of one another in their small sleeping quarters. They'd given up the chance for a normal life, like their friends at home all had. But the Moffatts never minded because they shared a common dream.

Now they were finally on the brink of the big time. They had toured Europe and Asia to the cheers of thousands of screaming fans, and were now headlining at huge outdoor concerts in the United States and Canada, the biggest entertainment markets in the world.

The secret to the Moffatts' success — besides their obvious talent — was teamwork. Their voices worked together as one — making a unique sound that only the blending of brothers' voices can create. And that's what made Scott, Clint, and Bob so wigged. Now Dave was walking away and going out on his own. With him gone, everything would change — especially their unique sound.

Beyond that, they couldn't help feeling a little betrayed.

But to Scott, Clint, and Bob, the biggest head-scratcher of all was that their dad was letting Dave get away with this.

But Frank had spoken. He'd given Dave his okay, and it didn't seem as though he were going to change his mind. There was no doubt about it. Dave was leaving the group. And there was nothing his brothers could do to stop him.

"Well, I guess we should start rehearsing," Scott suggested to Bob and Clint as he picked up his guitar. Dave looked at his brothers. But they refused to make eye contact. Instead, they turned their backs to him. Dave shrugged. There was nothing left to say. He walked backstage to start preparing his own act.

Chapter Five

As soon as Dave was gone, Scott began playing the opening to "Misery." It just seemed appropriate at the time. Bob and Clint joined in as he sang.

"Wait . . . wait . . . wait," Scott shouted as he stopped strumming his guitar. "That just doesn't sound right. The harmonies are all off."

"I sang my part the way we wrote it," Bob said.

"Me, too," Clint added. "There's nothing wrong with the way we're singing. It's just that we're missing Dave's part, so it sounds weird."

"Then we're going to have to rework the harmonies on every song we're planning on doing tonight," Scott told the others.

"Oh, man! That's going to take all afternoon. We're never gonna get into the park," Bob moaned.

"Maybe you guys won't, but I will," Clint said.

"I have a date with a contest winner in one hour. It's not something I can ditch."

Scott and Bob shrugged their shoulders. "If we only have an hour, we'd better get on it," Bob said finally. "We'll do the best we can, and hope it works out tonight."

"It may not matter," Scott sighed. "When the fans find out they're only going to see three-fourths of the Moffatts, they're liable to turn around and leave."

That made Clint really mad. "Are you crazy?" he scolded Scott. "Dave's leaving is not the end of this group. We've got all the talent we need right here!"

Scott shook his head. He hoped Clint was right. But deep down, he just couldn't be sure.

An hour later, a tall woman with short, curly brown hair and round wire-rimmed glasses appeared backstage. She waited impatiently for the guys to finish their number, looking at her watch and sighing. The moment they reached the final chord, she strolled purposefully across the stage and stopped just in front of Clint. She smiled brightly and extended her hand.

"Hi, I'm Jeannie Alexander, associate editor of *Teen Scream* magazine," she introduced herself. "Now don't tell me. I've looked at enough pictures of you guys to know just who you are. You're

Clint. You're Bob, and you're Scott." Jeannie looked around the stage. "Hey. Where's Dave?"

Clint gasped. The guys weren't ready to have the press find out about Dave's defection just yet. There was no predicting how their fans would react to the news. This had to be handled very carefully. Quickly, he changed the subject. "He'll be back soon," he fibbed as he looked around the amphitheater. "But more important, where's my date?"

"Oh, she's waiting in the backstage area," Jeannie assured him. "We have a photographer all set up to take pictures of the very first moment you two meet. Our readers would love to see the expressions on your faces. You'll like the photographer I'm sure. His name is Paul, and he's not intrusive at all. You and Teresa will really feel like you're on an actual date, and not on some photo shoot. Except, of course, when we need you to stop and pose for the cameras."

"Of course. Doesn't everyone stop mid-date to pose for pictures?" Clint teased Jeannie.

But the magazine editor didn't seem to get the joke. Clint sighed and changed the subject. "Well, what are we waiting for?" Clint asked excitedly as he started to walk backstage. "So tell me, Jeannie, what's Teresa like? Does she like roller coasters?"

Jeannie smiled. "She's almost as excited about

going on the Niagara Falls water slide as she is about meeting you," she told Clint. "Teresa is a total wild woman!"

Now Clint was really psyched. A girl who liked adventure! What more could he have asked for?

Clint walked backstage and looked around for Teresa. But there was nobody there except Paul, the *Teen Scream* photographer; Clint's stepmom, Sheila; and a gray-haired woman wearing a pair of jeans and a red blouse. Sheila and the woman were having a very animated conversation. Both seemed to be laughing and talking at exactly the same time.

"Where'd Teresa go?" Clint asked the photographer finally.

"She's right there," he replied.

"Where?" Clint asked, looking around again.

Paul pointed toward where Sheila and the woman were talking.

Clint's eyes bugged. *It couldn't be! That woman had to be at at least sixty years old!* Suddenly, Clint got it. This had to be one of his brothers' practical jokes — didn't it? Didn't it?

No, it didn't.

Jeannie put her arm around Clint and walked him over to the two adults. "Clint Moffatt," she introduced him, "this is Teresa Rodriguez."

The flash of the photographer's lights blinded Clint for just a second. His authentic surprise at meeting Teresa was now recorded forever.

"Uh . . . well . . . hi," Clint stammered as he reached to shake Teresa's hand.

"Nice to meet you Clint," Teresa replied with a grin. "I'm a huge fan of your music. I'll bet I'm your oldest admirer."

"Yes, ma'am," Clint admitted.

Teresa laughed at his honesty. "My granddaughter played your CD for me when I was visiting her one afternoon. I loved it so much I went out and bought it myself. I've played it so often I know the words to all of your songs. So my granddaughter thought it might be fun to enter my name in this contest. She never dreamed I would win! We were both really surprised when Jeannie contacted me."

Clint tried to muster a smile. But in the back of his mind, he was really upset. He knew his brothers were going to be merciless with their teasing when they found out about this one. Desperately he turned to Sheila. "Can I talk to you for a second?" he asked her. Then he smiled at Teresa. "I just have a quick question about the show tonight. It won't take a minute."

Clint dragged his stepmother to the other side of the stage, way out of Teresa's earshot.

"They can't make me go through with this thing, can they? I mean, she's a grandmother!" Clint whispered.

"Yes, they can," Sheila said. "You agreed to this contest. You've got to spend the day with

Teresa, and then bring her backstage before the show tonight."

"Oh, *man!*" Clint groaned. "I can't wait to hear what the guys are gonna say about this."

"Look, it might not be so bad," Sheila said sweetly. "She seems pretty cool to me. After all, she *is* a Moffatts fan, so we know she likes good music."

Clint shrugged. "I guess," he said. "Besides, it can't be worse than that rehearsal Bob, Scott, and I just went through!"

Clint walked over and sat down next to Teresa. "Do you want to go get a cup of coffee or some tea at the snack bar?" he asked her politely.

Teresa laughed. "Are you nuts?" she asked. "Why waste our time at the snack bar when we can ride the Triple Terror Roller Coaster?"

Clint gulped. "The Triple Terror? I saw that as we drove in. It towers over the whole park. And it goes upside down — really, really fast. Why don't we start with something a little calmer?"

"Why?" Teresa asked. She grabbed Clint by the arm and pulled him toward the park. "C'mon," she urged him. "Don't be such a chicken."

Chapter Six

Dave wiped a bead of sweat from his forehead as he stood behind his keyboard. He was trying to come up with a lengthy instrumental piano tune — something he had always wanted to try onstage, but his brothers had nixed as being too self-indulgent. But tonight was Dave's night, and he wanted the instrumental to be a real showstopper. Unfortunately, so far nothing he'd written had been up to the level of the things he'd put together with his brothers.

"Okay, one more time, from the top," he said to himself. In fact, Dave had been talking to himself all morning long. It made being alone on the stage seem less weird.

Dave had never been all by himself in a giant amphitheater before. The place looked massive. He stared out at the empty bleachers, and tried to imagine the seats filled with happy fans. And tried to think positively. Because this was an amusement park and the concert was open to all the patrons, there were bound to be people there who didn't often come to Moffatts' concerts, like little kids with their parents, and even some grandparents. Those people didn't even know there were *four* Moffatts. So, they might be more likely to accept things the way they were now. Dave could "wow" them right from the start.

The trouble was, how would the loyal Moffatts fans relate to Dave, now that he was a solo act? Dave had to admit that he was a little concerned that the teens who had been following his career with the Moffatts would see him as a deserter, the way his brothers had. If the fans gave him the same cold shoulder, the amphitheater could be pretty icy by the time he was through. Dave could *not* let that happen!

"I've really got to prove myself to those people tonight," he told himself.

But Dave knew he wasn't going to win anybody over if he didn't play some awesome music during the show. Which meant he had to rehearse. So Dave took his place at center stage and stood behind his keyboard. He placed his fingers on the black and white keys, tapped his foot three times, and started to play. His left hand leaped from chord to chord, while his right hand pounded out a heavy-duty rock melody. But within a few seconds, he stopped playing once again. His rhythm was slightly off, and the balance didn't seem right. This was not working.

While Dave was busy figuring out a new instrumental number, Bob and Scott walked up to the stage. They refused to even look at their brother. Clearly, as far as Scott and Bob were concerned, Dave was a traitor — to the group and to the family.

Scott picked up a small piece of paper that had been left on top of one of the amps. "Hey? What's this?" he muttered aloud. He looked down at the paper. There was a list of songs on it. "Bob, check this out."

Bob walked up beside his older brother and read from the paper. "'If Life Is So Short.' 'Frustration.' 'Say'n I Love You' . . . wait a minute. Is this his set list?" Bob pointed up toward Dave.

Scott didn't reply. Instead, he strolled over toward the electrical outlet and pulled the plug out of the socket. Instantly, the sound left Dave's keyboard.

"Hey! What'd you do that for?" Dave demanded.

Bob waved the set list in the air. "Is this yours?" he demanded.

"Yeah. It's my set list for tonight."

Scott shook his head. "Oh, no, it's not!" he told his younger brother. "These are Moffatts' songs."

"So?"

"So, the Moffatts are the only ones who can sing them," Scott retorted.

"I wrote part of every one of those songs," Dave insisted. "They're just as much mine as they are yours."

"Maybe so, but we worked on them as a group. Just like all our songs. And you're not walking off with them," Scott declared. "You want to be a solo act — write your songs solo, too. You're not using ours!"

"How'm I supposed to write a whole set of songs by tonight?" Dave asked.

"That's not our problem," Bob told him. "You can always use songs written by someone else — just be sure to get permission, and fill out the forms to send to the publishing company so the songwriter can get paid."

Dave sighed. "That'll take all afternoon. I'll never see any of the rides in this park."

"It's rough being the *charismatic* one, isn't it?" Scott joked sarcastically. "Well, we're off to ride the Triple Terror. Then we're going to walk around for a while to see if we can find Clint and his blind date. I'm dying to find out what she looks like."

Bob frowned. "Yeah. I'll bet she's hot. Some guys have all the luck!"

"When we get back we'll work on that ad for a

new keyboardist," Scott told Bob. "I promised we'd have it ready by tomorrow."

Dave stared at Scott in surprise. "You're hiring a new keyboard player?" he asked.

"Of course," Scott told him. "And Robert — our manager — is going to set up auditions."

"Robert's helping you do this?!" Dave exclaimed.

Scott nodded. "Hey, don't look so surprised, that's the kind of thing managers do."

"We don't want to have to redo every one of our arrangements. Besides, the group could use some fresh style," Bob added. "Well, see you later!"

As his brothers walked away, Dave tried to shrug off the surprise and sense of desertion that had suddenly come over him. He knew he had no right to feel like his brothers were being disloyal to him — *he'd* been the one to strike out on his own.

Speaking of which, Dave had to get working. He plugged his keyboard in again and picked up a pad of music paper. He figured he could write at least one new song by tonight — after all, he and his brothers had written some of their best music in a couple of hours. He just hoped that his personal creative juices were flowing today.

"I can write a short song," he reassured himself. "It doesn't have to be some big long thing.

Then I'll play the instrumental and two cover songs. Four songs is enough for an opening act, anyway."

Eventually, Dave decided that he'd have to go with the instrumental the way it was — imperfect, but at least it was something. Besides, he had to get working on a song with lyrics. Dave had a few sketches of poems he'd worked on when they were traveling on the bus. He kind of liked the one called *Sunflowers*. It was a really sweet love poem about a summer romance, that he'd never gotten around to showing to his brothers.

"Well, they'll hear it tonight," he said to himself as he pulled the romantic lyrics from his travel bag. He sat down behind the keyboard and tried to work out the first few notes of a summery ballad.

But as his fingers ran over the keys, Dave could tell he was in trouble. He'd never written a song completely on his own. His brothers had always been around to add a line here and there, or to create a harmony to go with his melody. Dave missed their input. He needed someone to say, "Did you try a C-sharp there?" Or, "Maybe you need to change the tempo." If he just had that kind of assistance, Dave knew he'd be able to get a song going.

But the stage was empty. Dave was on his own now.

"Maybe I'll just do a few cover tunes tonight," he muttered to himself. "I can fill out forms faster than write a new song. Besides, everyone likes songs by the Beatles or Aerosmith. I'll be a real crowd-pleaser."

"You want to grab a sandwich before we go on the ride?" Scott asked Bob as the two wandered in the direction of the Triple Terror. The guys didn't have to ask anyone for directions to the massive roller coaster. The huge maze of metal tracks and wooden planks stood high above the park. It didn't matter where you stood. If you looked up, you could see people riding upside down and hear their screams as their roller coaster cars whipped over the curves.

"You want to *eat* before we go on *that*?" Bob exclaimed. "Are you *nuts*? I don't want to lose my lunch in front of all these people! We'd never live it down."

Scott nodded in agreement. When most people had an awkward moment, it was over in an instant. But when the Moffatts did something embarrassing it inevitably wound up being reported in the newspaper, or on a TV entertainment news show, or being spread all over the world over the Internet. "How about a soda or something then?" Scott suggested.

"Okay. But then I think we should go on the Black Hole water slide instead of the Triple Terror. At least it doesn't go upside down. And it's kind of warm out here. I wouldn't mind getting wet on a water slide."

Scott looked around the lunch area. There only seemed to be one table empty — in the far corner on the left. "Go grab that table," he told his brother. "I'll get the drinks."

But by the time Scott returned, there was barely any room for him to sit. Bob was surrounded by a group of teenage girls.

"Hi, Scott. I made a few friends while you were on line," Bob told his brother. "This is Katharine, Tatiana, Alison, and Phoebe."

"Hi," Scott said as he squeezed on to the end of the bench beside Phoebe. He handed Bob a soda.

"Thanks," Bob said as he took the cup. "Where's the straw?"

"All out of 'em."

Bob shrugged and brought the cup to his mouth. As he drank, he felt something cold and wet running down his chin.

"What the . . ." Bob looked down to see rivulets of dark brown cola running down the front of his shirt. He examined the cup. Someone had poked holes in the paper, near the top of the container. The minute Bob had tilted the cup, the soda had dripped out through the holes.

"Gotcha!" Scott shouted between fits of

laughter. "I made my own dribble glass. You are a mess, bro."

"But this is a brand-new Hawaiian shirt! I bought it when we went to Honolulu on vacation." Bob groaned as he looked at the brown, stain-soaked palm trees on his chest. That made two times in a row that Scott had pranked him.

"Hey, I warned you that I would get back at you for that salt stunt you pulled," Scott told his brother.

Tatiana dipped a napkin into her club soda, and began dabbing the front of Bob's shirt. "Here, this should get the stain out," she said sweetly to Bob. Then she glared at Scott. "How *could* you?"

"Why would you want to play a mean trick like that on your own brother?" Alison agreed.

"Hey, he pulled one on me first," Scott tried to explain. "He opened the salt and . . ."

But the girls didn't want to hear it. They were too busy consoling Bob and trying to clean up the mess.

"You poor thing," Phoebe soothed Bob as she got up and walked around to his side of the table. "That shirt is so great. I've never seen one with colors like that. I hope your brother didn't ruin it."

"It is my favorite," Bob told her. "But I bet I can get the stain out when we get to a laundromat."

Scott watched as the girls all tried to comfort Bob — and ignored him in the bargain. The girls were smiling at Bob's jokes, running their fingers through his long brown hair, and even passing him their phone numbers. Scott sighed. Bob was definitely milking this shirt thing for all it was worth.

A little while later, after Scott and Bob said their good-byes to the girls and wandered off toward the water rides, Bob tucked the phone numbers into his shirt pocket, looked at Scott, and chuckled. "Remind me to thank you for that one, bro."

Scott didn't say anything. He just rolled his eyes.

"Oh, and one more thing," Bob added. "Be sure to watch your back. You never know when I might strike again. In fact, the only thing you know for sure is that I *will* get you, dude."

Chapter Seven

Scott and Bob weren't the only ones enjoying their day at Sugar Mountain. Clint had put the whole Dave situation out of his head while he rode on the roller coaster and other rides. That was because Teresa was barely giving him time to think as she dragged him from ride to ride.

"Whoa! I'm really dizzy!" Clint admitted as he stepped down from the Spinning Dinos ride. From the moment he and Teresa had gone off on their "date," Clint had been rushing from one ride to another. Teresa couldn't seem to get enough of the wild roller coasters like the Double Looper and the Triple Terror.

Clint had thought the Spinning Dinos would be a bit mellower than the others Teresa had chosen. After all, you just sit inside a dinosaur as it spins around a little bit. But what Clint didn't know was that inside each dinosaur-shaped car was a giant wheel, that the riders could turn to make the car spin faster.

Clint had started turning the wheel gently, but Teresa was having none of that. She grabbed the wheel with both hands and spun it with all her might. The car was turning so fast that outside the car the park looked like a giant blur.

"Oh, come on. We weren't going that fast," Teresa chided him. "I thought you were supposed to be the adventurous Moffatt!"

"So did I — until just now," Clint answered with a laugh. He had to admit he was having a really great time. Teresa had more energy than anyone Clint had ever met. She was funny, and she sure knew about music. She'd seen all the great stars in concert. She'd been to the Beatles concert at Shea Stadium, she'd seen the Grateful Dead about thirty times, and she'd even worked in the medical tents at Woodstock — the *first* Woodstock back in 1969. Teresa was more than glad to tell Clint all about how you couldn't really hear the Beatles at Shea, because everybody was screaming so loud, and the equipment back then was so lousy, anyway. And she told him about how at Woodstock she'd spent twenty minutes talking to some guy about the future of rock 'n' roll, and didn't realize until after he'd left that it was Roger Daltrey from The Who. Clint thought it was really cool that a woman who had heard Paul McCartney play bass, and grooved to Jimi Hendrix jamming on the national anthem, wanted to hear the Moffatts in concert. It made him feel like he was part of something really special.

"I can't wait to hear you and your brothers play 'Misery,'" Teresa said to Clint as the two finally took a few minutes to sit for a soda break. "Do you play it just like it is on the CD, or do you vary it a bit for concerts?"

Clint was about to explain to Teresa that *everything* was going to sound different at tonight's show because they were minus a certain keyboard player, but before he could utter a sound, their conversation was interrupted.

"I need to get a shot of you two on the Ferris wheel," Paul, the photographer, told Clint and Teresa. "I thought you might want a rest, but Jeannie insists that we have to get enough photos of you two to fill a three-page article. There's no line at the Ferris wheel now. If we hurry we can get right on and snap a few good pictures."

Clint relaxed. The Ferris wheel, a nice, *peaceful* ride. You just sit in the car and move slowly in a circle. How bad could it be?

But the minute he and Teresa climbed into the enclosed car, he knew he was wrong. Teresa didn't like any ride to be too relaxing. As the car gently started to glide up toward the top of the wheel, she began rocking her body back and forth on the seat. As she moved, the car rocked, too.

"Come on Clint, shake it with me!" Teresa urged.

So Clint followed Teresa's lead. It was scary moving back and forth like that when he was three stories off the ground, but Clint had to admit there was something exciting about it, too. Teresa had a way of making everything seem exciting. Clint couldn't wait to tell his brothers about the great day he was having.

HIS BROTHERS! For the first time since they'd met, Clint remembered that Teresa was a grandmother! No matter how cool a day he was having, he knew the guys were going to really rank on him this time.

But Clint pushed that thought away. Instead, he moved from side to side, and made the Ferris wheel car shake even harder.

While Clint and Teresa were busy rocking the Ferris wheel, and Bob and Scott were getting soaked on the Black Hole, Dave was toiling at the amphitheater, filling out the permission forms for the publishing companies. So far he'd decided to open with "Hey Jude" by the Beatles, because it could be done completely on the keyboard. He could follow that up with a keyboard version of Nirvana's "Smells Like Teen Spirit," and then he figured he'd give the crowd "Don't Want to Miss a Thing" by Aerosmith — for no reason other than Aerosmith was Dave's favorite group.

Dave didn't mind doing the forms himself. He just sort of wished that Robert, the group's manager, would have hung out while he filled them out. It wasn't that Dave needed help or anything, it was just that he was lonely. Of all the Moffatt brothers, Dave was the most sociable. Scott always said, "Dave'll chat up anybody, no matter who it is." And that was the truth. Maybe it was because Dave was a triplet. He'd never actually been alone — and had no way of finding out what that would be like. Or if he would take to it.

But solo was a synonym for alone. And Dave knew that. He also knew that going solo was his decision. He was going to have to take the good with the bad. Besides, being alone once in a while never hurt anyone . . . did it?

"I'll get used to this," Dave told himself. Then he frowned. "Oh, man, I'm talking to myself again!"

Dave had originally thought that he'd just have to fill in a blank here, and sign his name there, and the whole thing would be over. But there were so many questions on the forms. He was starting to feel totally overwhelmed. And not just because of the songs. He still had plenty to do before the concert.

While Dave was still with the Moffatts, his main responsibilities — aside from the music, of course — were to help develop a Moffatts merchandise line. It was up to him to determine which clothing companies or calendar makers would be the best to carry the Moffatts' name. He didn't have a whole lot to do with the day-to-day running of the concerts. That was more Clint's domain. Clint was the business-minded brother, and he loved making concert arrangements, whether it was figuring out when and where the equipment should be set up, how many security guards they would need, or what food would be served to the band and the crew. Clint even made sure that the wardrobe people had all of the guys' clothes pressed and ready for the show.

Clint made it all seem so easy. But just the thought of organizing all that for himself made Dave dizzy. And what made it worse was that Dave knew he wouldn't just have to plan this concert, he would have to take care of his entire career from now on. That meant that he would have to write all of his own material, prepare for all of his own concerts, take control over finding producers and directors for his own videos, and work with record producers and engineers.

And on top of that, he was going to have to find time to squeeze in his schoolwork.

Dave, like his brothers, was home-schooled,

which meant that the brothers had lessons and homework that were given to them by Sheila and their dad. Like all other 16-year-olds, Dave studied history, math, English, science, and music (of course!). But he did his work a few hours each day while the group traveled.

Although some people thought the Moffatts were missing out by not being part of a regular high school, Dave really liked being home-schooled. Sheila made learning interesting, and she was able to relate the work to the group's tours. Dave remembered one time when the guys were in Japan — they did a whole-earth studies lesson on the effects of global warming on rice farming. They even got to visit real rice paddies!

But no matter how much fun home-schooling could be, it still meant homework and studying. The brothers' education had to match up to Canadian national standards. So the guys had to send tests and homework assignments back to a government office in Canada, where their work was graded. Home-schooling was definitely not a "free ride."

Dave had a feeling that between his schoolwork and his new musical responsibilities, he wasn't going to have any time for a social life. And that was a total bummer — especially since girls were Dave's number-one priority — after music of course. Dave was a natural-born flirt!

But for the time being at least, the only girls

Dave was going to see would be sitting in the audience. As it was, he'd be lucky if he even got to go on one ride — alone — today.

Well at least I won't have to eat Mexican food for the nine billionth time, Dave thought to himself. When it was Clint's decision, the backstage dinner was usually tacos, burritos, and enchiladas. But now that Dave was a solo act, he was going to order up some Chinese food — that was *his* favorite.

"Well, if it isn't Mr. Solo Spotlight!"

Dave jumped as he heard Bob's voice booming from the rear of the amphitheater. "How's it going?"

Dave put on a fake smile. There was no way he was going to let Bob know just how tough this solo act thing was.

"Great!" he replied. "I'm just finishing up these forms, and then I'm going to have a sound check and a run-through. You want to stick around and listen?"

Bob shook his head. "Sorry. I'm just here to change my shirt — it's a little sticky. Then Scott and I are going to brave the Niagara Falls water ride. We figured a couple of Canadian guys like us owe it to the homeland to ride the falls — even if they're at Sugar Mountain Amusement Park instead of in Canada."

"Sounds like fun," Dave agreed.

"Has Clint been back here yet?" Bob asked.

"I'm dying to know what his 'win-a-date' friend looks like."

"Nope, not yet. No one's been here all afternoon, except for Robert and me."

"Oh, well, we'll meet her before the show when she comes backstage," Bob remarked as he threw a blue tank top over his head. "Have you been on the Black Hole water slide yet? Scariest ride I've ever been on. You can't see a thing, and you feel like you're going tip over any second. What's your favorite ride so far?"

"I haven't gone on any of them yet," Dave admitted. "But as soon as I finish with the sound check, and make sure my clothes are all set up, I'm going for it big time!"

"Better hurry up," Bob warned. "We go on in three hours."

Dave gulped. *Three hours?* How was he going to get everything finished in just three hours?

Chapter Eight

"Okay, I'm ready to try the Triple Terror!" Bob announced as he joined Scott once again. He slapped his older brother on the back. "Are you brave enough?"

"Am I ever?!" Scott agreed. "Last one there's a rotten egg!"

Bob was the first one to reach the line for the massive roller coaster. Scott stood behind him in line and looked up at the ride.

"Whoa! This thing's really high up there," Scott said. "When this ride is over, I am definitely buying one of those 'I Survived the Triple Terror' T-shirts we saw at the souvenir stand. I'll have earned — ow!"

Scott was interrupted by someone lightly smacking him on the back. He turned around to discover three giggling teenage girls.

"Sorry," one of the girls apologized.

"Um, it's okay," Scott replied.

But a minute later, Scott felt another smack. He turned around. Again, the girls were laughing.

"What's going on —?" Scott didn't even have to finish the question. The expression on Bob's face said it all. "There's a sign or something on my back, isn't there?" Scott asked the girls finally.

The smallest of the three girls wiped her brown bangs off her forehead and beamed up at Scott. "Sure is," she said in a thick southern accent. "It says 'smack me.' So we did."

Scott grimaced. Bob must've taped the sign to his back when he gave him that *friendly* slap on the back.

"Real funny, Bob," he said finally, as he tore the paper sign from his back. "I ran through the entire park with that thing on me."

Bob was laughing. "I told you to watch your back, didn't I?"

"Aren't you guys with the Moffatts?" one of the group of girls asked. She, too, had a deep southern accent.

Scott nodded. "I'm Scott, and this is my brother, Bob."

"We're so excited to meet y'all!" the girl exclaimed. "We're big fans, but we didn't know you were going to be here. We came to the park on vacation, and it was an added treat to find out y'all were going to be playin'."

Bob grinned. "I love the way you talk. What's your name?"

"Cherilyn. And these are my cousins, Betsy and Ilana."

"My brother is a little nervous about going on this thing . . ." Bob began.

"Speak for yourself!" Scott interjected.

"Anyway . . . do you think you girls might want to sit with us?"

Cherilyn smiled. "We'd love to!"

Finally, Scott, Bob, and the girls reached the front of the line. They hopped into their cars, and waited for the guy who was running the ride to walk by and lock them in tightly.

"So where are your other two brothers?" Cherilyn asked Bob as they waited for the ride to begin.

"Well, Clint is with a blind date he met through a publicity shoot, and Dave is . . ."

Bob never finished the sentence. The roller coaster car took off full force, shooting uphill, picking up speed as it went around a sharp turn and then flipped upside down for a split second before righting itself.

"AAAAHHHHH!" Bob screamed. "This is soooooo COOL!"

While his brothers were busy being scared out of their wits — and loving every minute of it —

Dave was still alone at the amphitheater, working out the kinks in his performance.

On the upside, the permissions to play the songs he'd chosen had come through quickly. *That* was great. But on the downside, Dave knew that an audience would be bored just watching him sit alone at the piano singing for half an hour. He wanted to be able to move around and interact with them, just to vary things a bit. But without a backup band, it would be impossible — *that* was a bummer.

"Hey Dave, how's it going?" Frank asked as he and Sheila stepped out onto the stage.

"Okay, I guess," Dave told his dad. "I'm just trying to figure out the best way to keep the audience interested — especially since I'm only playing four songs."

"So what have you come up with?"

"Well, I was kind of thinking about what that reviewer said about me being successful in any genre of entertainment. I mean, who says my act has to be all music, right? So, I've been trying to come up with a few jokes that I can spring on the audience, in between songs," Dave answered.

"Sounds interesting," Sheila mused. "You wanna try them out on your dad and me?"

"You wouldn't mind?" Dave asked.

"Of course not."

Dave smiled for the first time all day. He'd really missed having someone around to bounce ideas off. "Okay, here goes. I thought I would play 'Smells Like Teen Spirit' and then come up to the front of the stage and say something like, 'You know a lot of people have asked me why I left the Moffatts. After all, the group is so successful. Everyone keeps saying a bird in the hand is worth two in the bush. But I say, a bird in the hand makes it hard to blow your nose!'"

Dave waited for his dad and Sheila to start laughing. But they didn't.

"Well, how's this then?" Dave suggested quickly. "Did you hear the one about the guy who went to the doctor because cucumbers were growing out of his ears? When the doctor asked him how that happened, he answered 'I don't know. I planted carrots.'"

Frank cleared his throat. Sheila stared at her shoes in silence. As Dave looked out at them, he could feel nervous perspiration forming on his upper lip.

"Hey, don't worry, I gotta million of 'em," Dave joked, trying to imitate the old-time comics he'd seen on TV reruns. "What do you get when you cross a radio with a Buick?"

"What?" Sheila asked.

"Car-tunes!" Dave shot back. "And what do you get when you mix a skunk and a bank?"

"I don't know," Frank replied cautiously.

"Dollars and scents!"

Dave waited for his parents to roar at those two jokes. But there was dead silence in the amphitheater. "Not too funny, huh?" Dave asked finally.

Frank stood and walked up on to the stage. He put his arm around Dave. "Actually that skunk joke really stunk," he said with a smile. "No, seriously. It's not that the jokes were bad, necessarily. It's just that stand-up comedy is like anything else. It takes years of practice to get it right. You need to work on timing and material and presentation. You've got to take the time to develop your individual comic technique."

"I wouldn't give up on it, though, Dave," Sheila encouraged him. "Maybe you'll be able to try doing stand-up comedy one day. But for now at least, I think you should stick to what you do best — playing the keyboards and singing."

Dave sighed. "I guess you're right. And I practiced those songs enough. I guess I'll run out and try to catch a few rides before the show."

Sheila looked at her watch and shook her head. "'Fraid not, Dave," she said gently. "You've only got an hour until show time, and they open the gates in half an hour. You've got to go backstage and get ready for tonight. Your brothers will be here any minute."

"Oh, man!" Dave complained. "You've got to be kidding! I blew my whole day at Sugar Mountain!"

Frank looked his son straight in the eye. "What can I say, Dave? That's show biz!"

Chapter Nine

Forty-five minutes before show time, Scott and Bob walked into the dressing room trailer behind the Sugar Mountain amphitheater.

"Sorry we're late," Scott apologized to his dad and Sheila. "The line for the bumper cars took longer than we expected."

"That's all right," Frank told his sons. "You two have a little extra time tonight. Remember, there's an opening act."

Bob frowned. "How could we forget? Thanks to our *opening* act, our whole sound is going to change tonight. Where is Dave, anyway?"

Frank pointed to the rear corner of the trailer. It had been blocked off by a blanket hung over a clothesline. "He's behind there," the boys' father explained in a low whisper. "Go easy on him, you guys. Despite the way he may sound, I think he's really nervous. He's never done anything like this before."

"Well, whose fault is that?" Scott muttered.

Frank nodded. "I understand how you feel. But remember, no matter what happens to the group, we're all still a family. And that means we should try to cheer for one another."

Scott walked over and pulled the blanket aside. "What's this for?" he asked Dave.

"Don't you know how to knock?" Dave replied angrily.

"Knock on what?" Scott countered. "A blanket?"

"Well, you shouldn't just barge right into a guy's dressing room," Dave argued.

"Your what?" Scott guffawed. "*This* is your dressing room?" He looked around the small area that Dave had blocked off for himself. There was a mirror perched on a table. Dave's clothes were hung over a corner of the clothesline. His dinner — take-out Chinese food — sat in cartons on the floor.

"Well, it's the best I could do under the circumstances," Dave explained to Scott. "Eventually, I'll arrange for my own trailer."

"Your own trailer?"

Dave nodded. "I'm a solo act now. I need my space."

Bob walked over and rolled his eyes at Dave. "Don't you think you're taking this star trip thing a little far?" he asked his brother. "I mean, it was just *one* review in *one* newspaper. And your whole opening act is what — three or four songs?"

"For tonight, yes. But when I have more time, I plan on getting a whole act together. Or I might try to get a part in a movie. I've always wanted to be killed off by a whacked-out villain in one of those movies like *Scream* or *I Know What You Did Last Summer.*"

Before Scott and Bob could tell Dave what they thought of *that* idea, Clint came rushing into the trailer. He held a huge, green, plush dragon toy in his arms.

"Whoa! Where'd you get that?" Bob asked him.

"Teresa won it for me at the basketball toss," Clint said. "Isn't it awesome?"

"Aren't you supposed to be the one winning the toys for her?" Scott questioned Clint.

"I tried, believe me," Clint insisted. "But I really stink at those games. I couldn't get one ball to land in the bucket. And I was even worse at the darts booth. Teresa, on the other hand, was amazing at winning stuff! In fact, she was totally amazing at *everything.* She's not afraid of any ride — she didn't even hold on when the Triple Terror went upside down. And you should have seen her on the Twister. She screamed louder than anyone!"

Clint put the stuffed dragon down on the floor. His brothers stared at him, surprised. Clint's white polo shirt was covered in stains. Now, for anyone else that might be expected after a full day at an amusement park. But not for Clint. Clint was a total neat freak. He even folded his clothes before he put them in his laundry bag.

"Whoa!" Scott exclaimed. "What got all over you?"

"Mustard, ketchup, and a little relish I think. Teresa and I had a hot-dog eating contest."

Bob laughed. "Did she win that, too?"

Clint grinned. "Nope, I did. I ate four of them. But I'm not totally convinced that Teresa didn't let me win."

"So, when do we get to meet the wonder woman who got Clint Moffatt to stain his shirt?" Bob asked.

"She'll be here in fifteen minutes. *Teen Scream* wants to get some backstage shots of Teresa meeting you guys. But I told them we'd want to get changed in private first." Suddenly, Clint noticed the blanket hanging from the clothesline in the corner of the dressing room trailer. "What's that about?"

"Oh, that's Dave's private dressing room. Apparently he's too much of an up-and-coming star to share his space with us lowly Moffatts," Bob said sarcastically. "Man, he's really getting on my nerves."

Clint laughed, and got his yellow-and-white striped shirt and white slacks from his travel bag.

"You guys should've seen Teresa on that white rapids raft ride in the water park. She made us sit right in front so we would get really wet. She didn't even care if her makeup got runny or her hair got messed up."

Scott was impressed. "She sounds like a really cool girl."

Clint thought for a minute. "Well, I wouldn't exactly call her a *girl*," he said.

"What would you call her then?" Bob asked.

Clint didn't answer. He ran his fingers through his short brown hair, fluffed out the blond streaks in the front, and walked outside. "I'm going over to the catering table," he called out to his brothers, changing the subject. "Anybody want anything?"

"I'll come with you," Scott offered. "I need some water. Bob, you want a drink or something?"

"How about a lemonade? And please, no dribble glasses this time. I'm already dressed." Bob pointed to the blue tank top and khaki carpenter pants he'd just put on. He didn't look as snazzy as Clint did in his matching shirt and slacks, or as put together as Scott did in his shimmery gray slacks and white shirt (with only the bottom three buttons buttoned, as usual), but Bob's sleeveless shirt and loose pants were the best clothes there were for drumming.

Clint started laughing. "A dribble glass! You didn't?" he asked Scott.

Scott nodded. "Oh, yes I did. It was classic!"

"I'll bet," Clint agreed.

"Yeah, well, I got in a few intense pranks of my own," Bob defended himself.

"No doubt bro," Clint assured his identical twin. He turned and looked pleadingly at Bob and Scott. "Do you think you guys could call a truce now? We've only got a few minutes until Teresa gets here, and I'd prefer she meet my brothers while they're all in one piece. Besides, it's going to be hard enough to explain to *Teen Scream* that Dave has split from the band. I don't want them to think you two are feuding, too. That would look pretty bad."

There was no arguing with that kind of logic.

"I'll cool it if you will," Scott promised Bob.

"It's a deal," Bob agreed as he picked up a hairbrush and ran it through his long, thick, dark brown hair.

"Teresa sounds totally awesome," Scott told Clint as they walked outside. "She seems like she's full of surprises."

Clint nodded and chuckled to himself as he thought about how his brothers would react when they finally got a chance to check out his blind date. "Oh, I think Teresa will surprise you all right. I know I was totally shocked when I met her!"

Chapter Ten

Dave sat alone in his makeshift dressing room and listened to his brothers chatting. Scott and Clint had come back with the drinks, and they were waiting for Teresa to arrive. Now they were all kidding around, talking about the series of practical jokes Scott and Bob had obviously been pulling on each other all day.

Dave wanted to join the conversation, but he knew he probably wasn't welcome. His brothers hadn't exactly been his buddies today. Not that he could really blame them. They were obviously jealous. After all, the reporter hadn't even mentioned any of *them* by name.

Dave absentmindedly rubbed the small silver charm he wore around his neck. All the Moffatt brothers wore them. Frank had gotten one for each of his sons. He said that the charms were there to remind the guys to always think of God first, other people second, and themselves third.

Dave knew that his brothers probably felt he'd been thinking of himself first ever since that newspaper review had come out. And maybe he had been. But deep down, Dave knew he had to give this solo thing a try. *I don't want to wake up at age forty and wonder what might have happened*, he thought to himself.

Still, he wished there was a way he could do this solo thing without making it so hard on his brothers.

"Fifteen minutes, Dave," the stage manager for the Sugar Mountain amphitheater called as he poked his head inside the trailer. "We're opening the gates now."

"I'll be ready," Dave shouted back. Then he gulped. If he weren't mistaken, his voice had cracked just slightly as he'd answered the stage manager's call. What if he was getting laryngitis? There'd be no one up there to cover for him if he lost his voice right on stage!

Quickly, Dave sang a quick scale. "Do-re-mi-fa-so-la-ti." Whew! His voice sounded just fine.

"That your first number, Dave?" Clint asked, as he poked his head behind the blanket.

"Very funny," Dave replied.

Clint grinned. "Seriously, bro. We just want to wish you good luck. I mean, this isn't how we want it to be, but you're still our brother. So, knock 'em dead, okay?"

For the first time all day, a real smile passed

over Dave's lips. "Thanks," he told Clint sincerely. "I'll do my best. Is Teresa here yet?"

"Any minute. You want to come over to our side and meet her?"

Clint didn't have to ask twice. Dave moved the blanket aside and walked over to where his brothers had gathered.

There was a knock at the door.

"Are you guys decent?" Jeannie's peppy voice asked from the outside of the trailer. "We have some women here who can't wait to see you all."

"Bring 'em on!" Dave joked.

Jeannie opened the trailer door and walked in. She was followed by Paul, who was lugging all sorts of camera equipment. Teresa, and a girl who looked about fourteen, with long brown hair and dark piercing eyes, walked up the trailer stairs just behind Paul. Teresa was calm, cool, and collected. Her companion, on the other hand, looked absolutely petrified at the prospect of meeting the Moffatts.

"You must be Teresa. We've heard so much about you," Scott said as he walked over to the teenager. He held out his hand politely. "I'm Scott."

The teenager blushed and giggled nervously. Clint started laughing, too. "That's not Teresa," he corrected his older brother as he took the real Teresa by the arm and introduced her. "This is. Teresa, I'd like you to meet my brothers, Scott, Bob, and Dave."

For a moment, the three brothers just stared at Teresa and Clint. Paul's camera caught their looks of surprise for posterity. But the boys didn't even blink at the blinding light of the flash. They were in shock.

Finally, Bob broke the silence.

"You're Clint's blind date?" he asked incredulously.

Teresa nodded. "Yup," she assured him. "This is my granddaughter, Elena. Since she's the one who entered me in the contest, I figured it was only fair that she be my guest at the concert. I know that position is usually given to the contest winner's parent or guardian, but in my case, I figured we could make an exception."

Clint walked over and shook Elena's hand. "Thank you so much for sending in that entry form in Teresa's name," he said sincerely. "I can't remember having so much fun anywhere — or with any one!"

"You're welcome," Elena replied. "My grandmother *is* pretty cool. I don't think there's another person in the whole world quite like her."

"You think you three guys could wipe the shock out of your eyes?" Teresa chided Scott, Bob, and Dave. "You're making me feel like some sort of natural oddity."

The three brothers blushed furiously. "Sorry,"

Dave apologized. "I guess we just weren't expecting . . ."

"The gray hair really threw you, huh, Dave?" Teresa laughed. "It kind of throws me, too, every time I look in the mirror. The reflection says grandmother, but in my mind, I'm about fifteen."

"Actually you have more energy than any fifteen-year-old I've ever met, Grandma," Elena complimented Teresa.

"I'll say," Clint agreed.

"So tell me, what songs are you playing tonight? I'm hoping to hear 'Written All Over My Heart.' It's probably my favorite of your newer tunes," Teresa asked, changing the subject.

"Grandma's got all of your albums," Elena assured the Moffatts. "She even got her hands on the country ones you did when you were little. She says Christmas is just December twenty-fifth until we hear *The Moffatts Christmas* at least three times."

"No way!" Bob exclaimed.

"It's true," Teresa admitted. "But if you want me to be honest, I like your new sound better. Country's okay — in fact, I listen to a lot of it. But when I put on your latest CD I can hear that this is the kind of music you guys get into and believe in. That's why we fans can relate to it, too. And your sound is so fresh and different," Teresa told him. "The way the four of your voices blend together, sort of reminds me of some of the early songs the Beatles did. Take 'Twist and Shout.' That song only works because all four of the Beatles were singing the harmonies."

Dave gulped. Wait until Teresa found out that from now on there would only be three Moffatt voices in the family's harmonies.

"The Beatles are one of our biggest influences," Bob told Teresa. "Did you know that?"

"I think I read that in one of Elena's magazines," Teresa admitted.

"I'm sure it was her latest issue of *Teen Scream*," Jeannie reminded Teresa. "We printed that in our 'Twenty Things You Didn't Know About the Moffatts' article. I should know. I wrote that one."

Teresa winked at Clint. "Oh, *of course*," she agreed. "That must be it."

"Did I mention that Teresa actually heard the Beatles play live once — at Shea Stadium," Clint told his brothers.

"No way!" Bob exclaimed.

Teresa shook her head. "Well, I wouldn't exactly say I heard them. Nobody did. And I was sitting pretty high up — in the nosebleed seats in the stadium. So it's actually even an exaggeration to say I saw them. But I always tell everyone that the Beatles and I were in the same place at the same time. And any way you look at it, that's really cool."

Scott nodded excitedly. "Totally! Wish I'd been there."

Teresa laughed. "Then you'd be about as old as I am right now," she remarked.

"You're the youngest adult I know," Clint assured Teresa. "I had a tough time keeping up with you today." He turned and looked her gratefully in the eyes. "You know, you taught me an awful lot."

"You mean about how to throw a basketball with just the right amount of spin to have it land in a barrel?" Teresa joked.

"That, and how to knock down the rubber ducks with a water gun," Clint laughed.

"And how to eat four hot dogs and still get on the Twister without throwing up," Teresa reminded him.

Clint moaned and held his midsection, pretending to have a stomachache. Then he looked seriously at Teresa. "But above all, you taught me how important it is not to judge people by their age. I'll never forget that — or you."

The stage manager popped his head back into the trailer. "Five minutes, Dave," he called. "You'd better get ready to go on."

"Well, guys, that's my final warning. I've got to get going. It was nice meeting you, Teresa. Maybe I'll see you after the show."

Jeannie looked curiously at the brothers. "Why

is Dave the only one who is supposed to be on-stage? What's going on here?"

"Didn't anybody tell you?" Dave said. "I'm going out on my own. I'm going to be a solo act."

"When did this happen?" Jeannie asked, alarmed.

"I decided just this morning. This is my first gig."

Teresa and Elena looked shocked, and more than just a little upset at the idea of Dave leaving the group.

Jeannie, on the other hand, looked like she could burst. "Oh, man!" she exclaimed. "Clint, why didn't you tell me this news earlier? I could have written this story hours ago. It's so exciting! Wait until my editor back in L.A. hears about this. Dave Moffatt is going solo. It's the scoop of the year!"

Jeannie went right into work mode. She turned to Paul. "Get out there and take a few pictures of Dave's first solo outing. I'll write a quick story and e-mail it to the office. I'll need a few quotes from you, Dave, *after* your act, of course. If we can just talk for five minutes when you get off-stage then I'm sure we can get it all into the next issue. I'll need a set list, too, and . . . *O-o-o!* Dave I could just kiss you. This is the best news I've heard in ages!"

Scott winced. "That's not quite the reaction we had when he told us."

Dave smiled. "Definitely not. But it was exactly the reaction *I* was hoping for." He looked in the mirror and spiked his short brown hair a little higher, fixed the collar on his black button-down shirt, and smoothed the creases in his black jeans.

"Well, I'm off," he told the others. "Wish me luck out there."

Chapter Eleven

Dave walked out onto the dark stage. To reach his keyboard, he had to follow a path of glow-in-the-dark tape that had been placed along the floor of the stage. There was no curtain separating the stage from the audience, but the darkness of the theater was so intense he couldn't see a thing.

But Dave knew the audience was out there. He could hear them shouting, "Moffatts! Moffatts! Moffatts!"

Dave wondered if the audience knew he was going to be performing a solo act before his brothers went on. He figured that since the crowd seemed to be screaming for the group, they didn't have a clue. And that made sense, especially since there hadn't been any time for Dave to arrange for signs about his solo debut to be posted in the park. His new set was going to be a surprise to the fans. Dave had to wonder whether they were going to think of it as a great bonus or as a total disappointment.

As he took his place in the center of the stage, Dave was surprised that he didn't feel more nervous. Usually, just before the lights went up, Dave could feel butterflies flopping around in his stomach. The familiar feeling of stage fright didn't really bother him — especially since he knew that many great performers had suffered from nerves before a show. Besides, the slight stress usually got his adrenaline pumping.

But tonight, when he *should've* been nervous, Dave felt curiously calm. He stood behind his keyboard, and rested his fingers on the keys. His arms felt light and relaxed. He was so focused on that feeling that the sounds of the audience almost faded from his ears.

And then he heard the announcer's voice over the public address system.

"Ladies and gentleman, welcome to the Sugar Mountain amphitheater! Tonight, you're in for a special treat. It's the first-ever solo performance of one of the world's hottest young stars. Give it up for *DAVE MOFFATT!*"

A single, bright white spotlight focused on Dave as he stood behind the keyboard. If the fans in the audience were surprised to see Dave alone on the stage, they didn't show it. They jumped up, stomped their feet, and applauded wildly.

Dave just stood there.

The audience clapped even harder. A small cheering section started shouting, "Dave! Dave! Dave!"

But Dave didn't even acknowledge the fans who were calling out his name with love and enthusiasm. It's not that he didn't *want* to thank them for their warm reception. It was just that he *couldn't* thank them.

Dave was frozen on the stage.

A bead of sweat popped up on Dave's forehead and began dripping down the side of his face. He tried to wipe it away, but his hands wouldn't move.

Dave looked down at the black-and-white keyboard before him. Those keys, which he knew almost as well as his own face, now seemed like strangers to him. They were like giant shark's teeth, just waiting to chew him up whole. He couldn't remember what chords to play. The words to his songs had been erased from his brain. Not that it mattered. Dave couldn't sing anyway. He tried to sing, but his lips were too parched to open, and his tongue felt glued to the bottom of his mouth. Dave's eyes certainly weren't dry, however. They were welling up with tears of sheer panic.

After a minute or so, the audience began to sense that something was wrong. They quieted down and sat in their seats. A murmur of whispers spread through the arena, as the members of the audience tried to figure out if something was wrong with Dave.

As Dave stared into the crowd, he finally knew the meaning of the expression "deafening silence." The crowd seemed to be unraveling before his eyes. He even saw one father take his daughter by the hand and head for the exit.

Bob peeked out from behind the curtain and stared at his brother. "What's he doing out there? Is this some kind of joke?" he whispered to Clint and Scott.

"If it is, it sure isn't funny," Clint replied.

"I don't think it's a joke," Scott told Clint and Bob. "I think he's totally freaked out up there."

"So much for all that *charisma* and *charm*," Bob remarked sarcastically, referring to the newspaper review that had started this whole mess in the first place.

"We can't just let him bomb out there . . . can we?" Clint asked.

Scott shook his head. "Remember what Dad said? No matter what, we're a family. I think we have to go out there and save Dave's — and the Moffatts' — reputation."

"But how are we going to explain *this*?" Bob asked. "He's just standing there!"

As Scott looked at Bob, an idea popped into his head. "That's it!" he exclaimed.

"What's it?" Bob asked him.

"Just follow my lead," Scott assured him with a grin. He picked up his guitar and got ready to head out onto the stage. "Are you guys ready for 'Operation Save Dave'?"

"What choice do we have?" Clint replied with a nod.

"I'm in," Bob agreed.

And with that, the three remaining Moffatts took the stage behind their brother, Dave.

"So, how'd you like our little practical joke?" Scott shouted out to the audience.

"My favorite kind of prank!" Bob agreed, laughing, as he sat down behind his drums. Bob was impressed with his older brother. That was quick thinking!

"You guys didn't really think Dave here was splitting up the act did you?" Clint asked the audience.

Once again, the crowd leaped to its feet, screaming out a resounding "NO WAY!"

Dave still couldn't seem to move his arms and legs, but he was able to move his eyes enough to see that his brothers were now on stage and ready to play.

"Now let's start this show for real!" Scott cried out.

Bob banged his drumsticks together in the air. "One, two, a-one-two-three-four!" he called out to his brothers as he gave them the downbeat.

As the guys continued singing "Frustration,"

Dave realized suddenly that he was playing music. Not only that, he was singing harmonies, and moving his body around. Somehow, having his brothers on stage with him had brought Dave back from the land of absolute terror that he'd been in when he'd taken the stage alone.

As the guys jammed, Clint looked out in the audience. From the corner of his eye he caught a glimpse of Teresa in the front row. She was standing up and leading her section of the amphitheater in a giant human wave. As the audience members rose and sat in their seats, the wave of bodies made its way around the entire arena. Clint looked over at Scott. He was grinning. Scott had obviously seen Teresa's action, too. The brothers nodded approvingly at Teresa. No doubt about it, she was the ultimate Moffatts fan.

As the Moffatts played the final chords of the song the audience went wild. There were close to 2,000 people in the crowd, and their applause sounded like giant claps of thunder rushing back onto the stage. The Moffatts had taken over Sugar Mountain! In fact, the only person who wasn't focused on the stage was Jeannie. She was standing off to the side, frantically typing into her laptop computer. Obviously, she was making some changes to her big scoop about Dave leaving the band.

As the guys took a bow, Dave put a hand over

his mike and shouted to his brothers. "Thanks for saving my neck. I owe you guys, big time."

Clint nodded. "You have no idea *how* big time!" he agreed.

Scott waited for the cheers to die down. Then he stepped back up to microphone. "Hello out there!" he shouted. "We're the Moffatts!"

The crowd roared wildly.

Bob started playing a steady, pounding drum-beat from the back of the stage.

"On the drums, we've got the rhythm-meister himself, Mr. Bob . . . Moffatt," Scott announced to the crowd.

Bob kept up the beat while Dave joined in on his keyboards, playing a complicated combination of chords and notes, which added a melody line to the rhythm section. "On keyboards, we've got the wild man, Mr. Dave . . . Moffatt!"

Clint added a pulsating bass riff to the mix. "And over here on bass, we've got the soul man, my fellow Canadian, Mr. Clint . . . Moffatt!"

By now, the audience had picked up the beat. The fans were clapping and stomping their feet to the rhythm that Bob and Clint had created.

That was Clint's cue. He leaned in toward his mike and announced, "Over there on guitar is our older brother. He's the one we call Elvis. Ladies and gentleman, Mr. Scott . . . Moffatt!"

As soon as all the guys were jamming together,

the audience could no longer control their excitement. Girls were dancing in the aisles. Some fans threw bouquets of flowers at the stage. A single red rose landed on Dave's keyboards. He picked it up, put it between his teeth, and clapped his hands in the air as though he were doing a Spanish flamenco dance.

Some girls in the crowd even tried to rush onto the stage in the hopes of grabbing a quick kiss from their favorite guy. But security was too fast for them. The girls were pulled away from the Moffatts, helped down the stairs on the side of the stage, and asked politely to return to their seats.

No doubt about it, the energy level was high inside the amphitheater. And the guys were determined to keep things hot! So they kept on playing, and eventually morphed their free-form jam into the opening of "Raining on My Mind."

The audience was so involved with the show that they all started singing along with the brothers. And by the time the guys got around to the song's chorus, it was hard to tell where the Moffatts' voices began and the crowd's left off.

As the song came to an end, the Moffatts moved to the center of the stage and applauded the audience.

"You guys are awesome!" Clint congratulated them. "When are you cutting *your* album?"

The crowd erupted into a burst of laughter and applause. Clint waited for it to quiet down. Then he stepped up to his microphone once again.

"There's someone special here tonight," he told the crowd. "She started out as my blind date, and has wound up being a friend to all four of us. She's living proof that numbers don't mean anything. It's not how old you are, but how old you feel. Teresa, this one's for you. When it comes to fans, you are totally the 'Girl of My Dreams'!"

Chapter Twelve

After the concert, the Moffatts sat outside the amphitheater behind a black wooden table and signed autographs for their fans. Some of the girls had brought copies of the Moffatts CD to sign, but others were more original, asking the guys to write their names on T-shirts, sneakers, backpacks, and stuffed animals they'd won at the park.

"I didn't know you were an actor, too," one teen told Dave as he signed her Moffatts CD.

Dave looked up at her curiously. "What do you mean?"

"Well, you really had my girlfriends and I fooled for a minute there. We honestly thought you'd gone solo — and that you had real stage fright. But now that I think about it, that could never happen. You would never break up the group."

Dave blushed. "No, I would never do that," he assured her.

Dave didn't say a word to his brothers as they met with the teens who had come to hear them play. And his brothers didn't mention Dave's disastrous "debut," either. But when the last of the fans drifted off into the night, Dave turned to Scott, Bob, and Clint, and smiled gratefully.

"You guys really came to my rescue," he told them. "And I don't know why. I really acted like a jerk today."

Clint, Scott, and Bob didn't say a word.

"Well, aren't you going to say anything?" Dave demanded.

Clint shrugged. "No. I think the word 'jerk' pretty much says it all," he teased. "Forget about it. We covered your back, and one day, you'll cover ours, okay?"

"Yeah, that's what brothers are for," Bob agreed. "Hey, we all make mistakes."

Just then, Frank and Sheila walked up to the guys.

"We're pretty proud of you three," Frank told Clint, Bob, and Scott. "What you did for your brother on that stage was really terrific."

"Not to mention quick thinking," Sheila said. "Where'd you ever come up with that stuff about practical jokes?"

Bob looked at Scott. Scott stared at the floor. He knew if he looked at Bob he'd burst into hysterics, just thinking about the look on his brother's face when he sipped that salt-filled ice tea.

"Just popped into my head I guess," Scott finally muttered to Sheila.

"Guys, I'm really sorry," Dave apologized. "I don't know why I listened to that reporter. You'd think by now I would have realized not to buy into the hype. Making music with you guys is where I belong. It's what the fans like, and it's what I like, too."

Frank put his arm around Dave's shoulders. "I guess you discovered that making music with your brothers makes you happier than being alone in the spotlight," he suggested.

Dave nodded. "I just wish it didn't have to be such an embarrassing discovery," he sighed. Suddenly, he realized why his dad had been so quick to give him permission to go out on his own. Frank had wanted him to learn this lesson. "You knew I was going to bomb out there, didn't you?" he asked him finally.

Frank sighed. "If I had told you that you weren't ready to go out on your own, you would've argued with me, and quoted that review. And if I had suggested that the reason the Moffatts' music is so unique is that you and your brothers bring out the best in one another, you never would have believed me — at least not the way you were thinking at the time." Frank put an arm around his son and looked sincerely into his eyes. "But Dave, I want you to know that I never wished you would go out there and freeze like that. I guess I hoped you would figure it out *before* you went onstage. And when you didn't, then I decided to just hope for the best — whatever that might be."

"I guess you never figured on me being so stubborn," Dave admitted.

Frank laughed. "Look, at least the audience never knew you were really scared, and the band came together at the last moment. Still, I'm sorry you had to go through that tonight, son."

Just then, a woman with short black hair sauntered over to where the Moffatts were standing. She extended her hand and smiled right at Clint.

"Hi, there. I'm Elizabeth McDonough," she introduced herself. "And I have to say that I thought your performance tonight was brilliant — absolutely brilliant. Just like the one you gave in Bordentown."

"You saw the show in Bordentown?" Clint asked.

"I certainly did. And I loved it," Elizabeth assured him. "In fact I drove all the way here to Carlisle to hear you play again. I hit so much traffic, I didn't even get here until you were into your second song. But I'm glad I made it. I wanted to see if my first impression was right, and it was. You guys were really on tonight."

"Which Bordentown show did you catch?" Scott asked.

Elizabeth smiled. "I heard about what you did

for the fans that night. Giving them a show in the parking lot showed real class. But I was at the press show," she replied. "I'm with the *Bordentown Courier-Post.*"

"*The Bordentown Courier-Post*," Bob blurted out. "Wasn't that the paper that said Dave . . ."

"We, um, have to get going," Scott interrupted him. He didn't want to risk the chance of Elizabeth saying something that might start Dave thinking about going out on his own again.

"I *really* thought you were spectacular, Dave," Elizabeth remarked — as she looked squarely at *Clint.*

Clint stared curiously at Elizabeth and pointed to himself. "Me?" he asked.

"Of course," Elizabeth replied. "I noticed you from the start. You're a brilliant musician."

"Thank you for the compliment," Clint said. "But I'm not Dave. He is."

Dave smiled at Elizabeth and waved.

Elizabeth looked from Clint to Dave and blushed deeply. "Oh, this is so embarrassing," she admitted. "You both have short hair, and I guess I got confused when Scott introduced you. Obviously, I'll have to print a retraction to my review. I guess it was Clint here who caught my eye." Elizabeth smiled sweetly at the three other brothers and added quickly, "Naturally, I think you're *all* wonderful artists. But Clint has that certain something that cannot be ignored."

"Yeah, we find him hard to ignore, too," Bob joked. "Which is not to say we haven't tried."

Scott, Bob, and Clint all laughed at that one, but Dave was too confused to laugh. He felt as though someone had punched him in the stomach. Here he'd been a total jerk to his brothers, and almost made a complete fool of himself in front of 2,000 people, and he'd done it for absolutely no reason. That reviewer hadn't even been talking about him. As far as she was concerned, it was *Clint* who had all the charisma and charm.

"I'm glad you liked my music," Clint thanked Elizabeth. "Actually, I've been working on my own to write a couple of new songs recently."

Elizabeth practically glowed with delight. "O-o-o, I'd love to hear them," she suggested to Clint. "You know, I think you have real potential as a solo act."

Before Clint could utter a single word in reply, his brothers grabbed him by the collar and began dragging him back toward the dressing room trailer.

"It was nice meeting you, Elizabeth!" Scott shouted back to the dumbstruck reporter. "But we've gotta run!"

Dave looked over at Clint. *Uh-oh.* He recognized that familiar glint in his brother's eyes. It was a dangerous sign — as Dave should know.

"Don't even think about going off on your

own," Dave warned his brother. "Take it from one who knows. Stick with the group. It's the only way to go."

"I'm not going anywhere!" Clint assured his brothers. "The Moffatts are all for one and one for all!"